Words to Know Before You Read

across

Appleseed

carried

Johnny

sailed

shared

walked

www.rourkeeducationalmedia.com

Edited by Precious McKenzie
Illustrated by Ed Myer
Art Direction and Page Layout by Renee Brady

Library of Congress PCN Data

Johnny Appleseed / Anastasia Suen
ISBN 978-1-61810-168-6 (hard cover) (alk. paper)
ISBN 978-1-61810-301-7 (soft cover)
ISBN 978-1-61810-423-6 (e-Book)
Library of Congress Control Number: 2012936770

Rourke Educational Media
Printed in the United States of America,
North Mankato, Minnesota

*Scan for Related Titles
and Teacher Resources*

rourkeeducationalmedia.com

customerservice@rourkeeducationalmedia.com • PO Box 643328 Vero Beach, Florida 32964

Johnny Appleseed

By Anastasia Suen
Illustrated by Ed Myer

A Sing and Read Book
(Sing to the tune of The Muffin Man)

Oh, do you know the apple man,
the apple man, the apple man?

Do you know the apple man,
Johnny Appleseed?

John Chapman

CIDER

He carried seeds
across this land,
across this land,
across this land.

He carried seeds across this land,
Johnny Appleseed.

He sailed the rivers
across this land,
across this land,
across this land.

8

He sailed the rivers across this land,
Johnny Appleseed.

He walked in the woods across this land, across this land, across this land.

Woods

He walked in the woods across this land, Johnny Appleseed.

He planted seeds
across this land,
across this land,
across this land.

He planted seeds across this land, Johnny Appleseed.

He cared for his trees
across this land,
across this land,
across this land.

He cared for his trees across this land, Johnny Appleseed.

He shared his trees
across this land,
across this land,
across this land.

He shared his trees across this land,
Johnny Appleseed.

His apples grew
across this land,
across this land,
across this land.

His apples grew across this land,
Johnny Appleseed.

We eat apples
across this land,
across this land,
across this land.

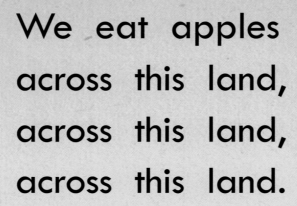

We eat apples across this land,
thanks to Johnny Appleseed.

After Reading Activities

You and the Story...

What did Johnny Appleseed do in America?

How did he travel across the land?

Why is it important that he planted seeds and trees?

Have you ever planted a seed or a tree?

Words You Know Now...

Some words have "ed" at the end to show past tense. Sometimes we just add it. Sometimes we change the word before we add it.

carry   carried   share   shared
sail   sailed   walk   walked

Can you find the three words that just added "ed" at the end?

across   Appleseed   carried
Johnny   sailed   walked

You Could... Plant Your Own Apple Tree

- Cut an apple open to see the seeds.

- If you cut it across the middle you will see a star.

- Take out the seeds.

- Dry your seeds.

- Find a nice sunny spot.

- You can plant the apple seeds in pots.

- Water them.

- Watch them grow!

- Move the trees into your yard when they get bigger.

About the Author

Anastasia Suen has taught kindergarten to college level students. The author of over 100 books for children, she lives with her family in Plano, Texas.

Meet The Author!
www.meetREMauthors.com

About the Illustrator

Ed Myer is a Manchester-born illustrator now living in London. After growing up in an artistic household, Ed studied ceramics at the university but always continued drawing pictures. As well as illustration, Ed likes traveling, playing computer games, and walking little Ted (his Jack Russell).